PUPPET SHARK
THE NOVELIZATION

CAT VOLEUR

BASED ON THE ORIGINAL SCREENPLAY BY
JANET HETHERINGTON
AND
TREVOR PAYER

Encyclopocalypse Publications
www.encyclopocalypse.com

Contents

Foreword
By Brett Kelly

Puppet Shark started as a silly idea for a movie. My wife makes puppets as a hobby. Since I make movies, it only made sense to make a puppet movie. People seem to want me to make shark movies..boom. Puppet Shark!

Now the movie is a novel? *Why?* WHY NOT? One silly idea begats another silly idea.

Want to read a book about a movie full of puppets?

You should.

And I guess you are since you are reading this.

Have fin!

Brett Kelly
Director, Puppet Shark
April 2024

Praise for Puppet Shark: The Novelization

"Cat Voleur rides a stuffed shark through the plush of the fourth wall to send you REELing into a fabric sea of dentists and Shakespearean verse."

— Damien Casey, half puppet and author of 28 Days Sassier

"Deft and delightful, this book made me laugh out loud. Voleur nailed it."

— Ruth Anna Evans, editor of OOZE: LITTLE BURSTS OF BODY HORROR

"Who doesn't like a shark story?"

— Grayson, puppet

"Incredibly charming and silly in the best way."

— Lor Gislason, author of Inside Out

"Cat Voleur's *Puppet Shark* is the *Moby-Dick* of novelizations of movies about murderous puppet sea creatures. But unlike *Moby Dick,* you won't want to skip a single word."

— Michael W. Phillips Jr., editor of This World Belongs to Us and co-editor of Escalators to Hell

"I've had enough. I'm not scared, and I don't believe a word of your dopey story."

— Chance, puppet

"While the movie Puppet Shark is as silly and lightweight as the puppets who populate it, the novelization by Cat Voleur really fleshes (or is that felts?) out the story in ways that makes it even better. Still silly and lightweight, but with added texture, pun fully intended, that makes the story even more fun."

— Robert Clark, host of the Creepy and Geeky podcast

"As I'm sure you've heard, this is a fintastic experience. The romance. The tragedy. The hilarity. Cat Voleur was meant to bring us shark movie novelization insanity. I'm circling for another bite!"

— Angel, from Voices From the Mausoleum

"There could have been more shark in this."

— Me, Fisherman Fred

"Puppet Shark is a ridiculous romp of a story. Cat Voleur has written a book that is fun to read, with tons of puns and a surprisingly complex narrative, topped with a twist that came as a complete - and a welcome! - surprise. Who knew that a book about a movie about puppets and their sharks would pack such a punch? Not me! But it sure does!"

— Cassandra Daucus, author of *Real Life Sucks Losers Dry*

From Your Author, Cat Voleur

Dear Readers,

Before you dive into *Puppet Shark: The Novelization*, I just want to set it up for you. There will be no spoilers here. I say that because I know when I'm reading a book, I get sort of wary about introductions. How many times have I read an introduction by a famous author only to have them spoil the end of their own book? Or worse, someone else's book.

Well I'm not a famous author, and you don't have to worry about any of that pretentious stuff from me.

Honestly, I am mostly writing this to thank you.

Puppet Shark: The Novelization has been a dream of mine, in a weird way, for longer than the movie *Puppet Shark* existed. I've been a fan of SRS Cinema for a long time, and a fan of shark movies even longer, and basically since I started writing I knew I wanted a novelization in my portfolio.

I love that novelizations, much like low-budget shark movies, seem to be having a moment. There was a time where they were sort of looked down on by literary snobs, but I have always loved them. They bring together my love of movies and my love of books, and often I feel like there is more to explore with the characters than what we get to see on the screen.

I always thought that if I got to do a novelization, I'd want to make the book grittier than the movie. I thought I'd clean up all the things I didn't like or understand about the film, and get really into the characters' heads. I imagined full backstories and elaborate secret plots that would spin out into these long epics in my head.

Then, I was lucky enough to get *Puppet Shark* as what is hopefully the first of many novelizations. *Puppet Shark* was the movie I got to adapt for the written word, and this might sound like a joke, but I was very blessed in that regard. It's not that it's a perfect movie, exactly, it's that the little flaws and stumbles are what make the movie so endearing to me. There are inconsistencies and awkward moments and it's objectively ridiculous, which I think is exactly why I didn't want to smooth over or correct a single thing about it.

My mindset for this novelization was instead, very much, to preserve the original project in as much detail as I could muster. I altered only a couple lines for the script where I absolutely had to for the format, and did my best to elaborate only at times where I felt my book was lacking from the loss of all the amazing visual gags.

There is so much love in my heart for this movie, and The Kelly Collective for creating it. A big thanks to them, and to Ron Bonk at SRS Cinema for letting me be a small part of this madness.

This script felt really out of my depth in some ways. I usually write really messed up horror with a lot of blood and swearing and psychologically upsetting characters. I've never done a novelization, but

I've also never done a comedy — or anything approaching appropriate for my family to read. I have a lot of very young cousins and very squeamish aunts who can only support me lovingly from afar.

But thanks to you, reading this, I have the chance to try things that are outside of my comfort zone. I would never have made it this far if it weren't for readers and my colleagues and my friends who —

CHOMP!

Prologue
Guy Has the Best (and Worst) Day of
His Life

Guy was a puppet in love. Well, mostly he was a puppet asleep, but the moment that his alarm clock went off, he was wide awake, and back to being a puppet in love.

"Today's the day!" he exclaimed, his heart filled to the brim with warm fibers at the thought. Even his dreams had been of Betsy-Sue, his love, and the hope that today would be a very special day for the two of them.

"I can't believe I'm actually doing this!"

He sat up, still trying to come to terms with his excitement. As you know, this can be very hard for any puppet. Leading doctors today largely suspect that a puppet is 90% excitement to 10% hand, and sometimes that can be a lot for felt to contain. "This is gonna be awesome!"

Even that was not enough.

"Oh my gosh!"

But that wasn't enough either. Guy was still really excited.

"I'm imagining it right now!"

And he *was* imagining it.

"Oh my gosh," he said again, and his fantasy of

the situation got even better. "Oh. Oh, I can't believe it!"

I don't need to tell you this, but he *couldn't* believe it.

"This is gonna be a dream come true!"

It would literally be a dream come true, because Guy had dreamed about Betsy-Sue every night since they met. Just moments ago he'd had a sort of waking daydream about her, when I described him imagining all that stuff before.

"Today is finally the day I've been waiting all month for this."

Now.

I know what you're probably thinking. You, reader, with your human brain. You're probably wondering, "Hey, isn't that sort of a weird thing to say? Isn't that a peculiar way to phrase it?"

If you're one of the more grammar critical readers, you might even be thinking it was a *mistake*. That I meant to type something else with my clumsy little puppet fingers. You're probably thinking something along the lines of, "Aren't you missing a punctuation mark in there somewhere?" or, "Good try, buddy."

To that I say simply, listen.

This may not be the book for you.

This is a book about *puppets*. And *sharks*. And the titular *puppet shark*.

I'm happy to take you on this ride, but the first thing you need to understand is that this is how puppets talk. We get excited. We combine phrases. We have a very non-critical, "laissez-faire" approach to our vernacular that gives it a certain, ad-libbed quality. It isn't, "Today is finally the day! I've been waiting all month for this!"

It's not, "Today is finally the day I've been waiting all month for! This!"

It's certainly not the calm, more literary and de-mure, "Today is the day. I've been waiting all month for this."

With a period? Instead of an exclamation point? No. No!

The words out of Guy's mouth, verbatim, were, "Today is finally the day I've been waiting all month for this!"

So why don't you pipe down and let the literal, actual puppet here tell you the story exactly as it happened? Shut your brain off for awhile, and let the expert narrate.

What were we talking about?

Oh, right. Guy.

"Yes!" he exclaimed, because he was still excited. But we were just getting to the part where he'd gotten some of it out of his system and was gradually starting to calm down. Even though he was still excited about Betsy-Sue and taking things to the next level, he was climbing down from his joyful jubilance enough that he could get out of bed and do something with the energy.

"Ahhhh," he sighed, for it felt good to have let that all out of his system. He looked around, but found himself unable to focus on anything.

There was only blackness as far as his puppet eyes could see.

"I can't see!" he exclaimed.

It was not terror that gripped him exactly. The darkness could never be as scary as the things Guy was actually afraid of, like playing poker, or going to the dentist, or losing his beloved Betsy-Sue. He was pretty sure she would still love him if he were blind, but he wasn't sure how he would get through life if he could never see her lovely, lavender face again. Fortunately, the eye mask fell off his face and restored his vision before he found the phone to dial up his best friend.

* * *

Grayson answered the phone.

"Dude, it's me!" The deep voice on the other end was clearly excited about something.

"Yeah," Grayson answered from where he relaxed on the couch. He was still a little sleepy. 8:00 is pretty early for a puppet on the weekend, and it was hard to work up enthusiasm for a conversation when you were missing cartoons.

"Today is the day! I'm going to do it. I'm going to propose to Betsy-Sue!"

"Cool."

"Yep! I got the ring and everything. Yeah, I know they say you got to save up about three months' salary to pay for the ring, so that's what I did!" He sounded proud of himself for a moment, and Grayson didn't have time to think of anything to say before he was going again. "It took me forever to get that ring out of the claw machine!"

"Yeah."

There was an awkward pause between the two puppets, where this man was clearly waiting for his best friend in the whole world to say something supportive. Grayson was not that man, but that just wasn't going to bring Guy down on such a special day.

"Anyway, wish me luck! I'm so excited. I really hope she says yes! See ya!"

"You got the wrong number," Grayson told him finally, and after a pause, the line went dead.

* * *

Guy was not about to be deterred by the phone call. He wanted to look his absolute best for Betsy-Sue. He took a good look at himself in the bathroom mirror after pulling on a (relatively) clean, striped tank top that looked beach appropriate.

His blue skin looked, well, blue, and his orange hair was more orange than ever. He patted it down with both hands, which had no noticeable effect, but made him feel considerably better.

He tested his breath, which honestly, wasn't great. He tested it two more times just to be sure, but came to the conclusion that it wasn't about to get better on its own.

He brushed his teeth — mostly his lips — and after some brief consideration he ran the toothbrush through his hair as well.

Again, to the human readers, I have to remind you that this is normal. Probably. That's how I assume toothbrushes work for all us regular puppet humans. Felt teeth are not so different in texture from our soft puppet hair that we definitely all have.

A pair of sunglasses completed the look, and Guy was feeling good enough about his reflection to give himself a big thumbs up. This did not look, from the outside, so terribly different from him just standing there with his arms out — but our complex language of gestures is really about the vibes.

* * *

Betsy-Sue could tell as Guy came rolling down the street that he had been smiling his wide, open-mouthed smile the whole way over. That was something she rather fancied about him — how easily excitable he was.

She was waiting just outside her house, a beach

bag in one hand and a parasol in the other. Her parasol was really just an umbrella, and to be honest, she wasn't sure what the difference was. She was really counting on Guy not knowing the difference either, because while it was silly to bring an umbrella to the beach, it felt totally practical — maybe even a little sophisticated — to bring a parasol. She was going to be having her picture taken soon, and the last thing she wanted was for her beautiful, smooth felt to get faded in the hot glare of the sun.

"Come on, Betsy-Sue!" he called to her as his little plastic car pulled to a stop in front of her home. "Let's get going!"

She found herself returning his open-mouthed smile as she climbed into the car with all her things, and helped him drive it to the beach.

* * *

The beach was expansive, with sandy sand and blue, stationary water in the distance.

Guy thought that Betsy-Sue looked absolutely stunning. Her long, auburn locks fell over her square shoulders, as she was wearing a bikini unlike any he had ever seen. It looked perfect with her crocheted sun hat.

You really need to understand how beautiful she was.

She had eyelashes.

She was eyelash-having, perpetual lipstick-wearing, pure puppet pretty.

It seemed impossible that she was there on the beach to spend time with him.

"Oh Guy," she sighed blissfully. "I'm so glad you asked me to come to the beach." Betsy-Sue looked around at the scenery as she expressed her gratitude, but Guy found he could only look at her. "It's such a beautiful day."

"Yeah," he said, completely missing an opportunity for a romantic line he had seen in a movie and had been wanting to try. "And I've got something special planned."

"You do?" He loved how her round, still eyes could convey so much excitement through the frequent and emphatic throwing back of her head. "What's that?"

"I rented out a boat." It didn't sound that special to say out loud, even though it was supposed to. But he couldn't tell her about the other part that was supposed to actually make it special, and so he just kept talking. "You, me, alone on the boat."

Her mouth opened so wide that it obscured her cute little nose. She opened it and closed it several more times in surprise before finding the words to express herself.

"Oh my goodness! How romantic!"

She looked to him, and he looked back at her. Their eyes locked as the sound of invisible waves crashed loudly over the horizon.

"Ready to go for a ride?" he asked.

"Absolutely." She paused. "Where do we go?"

Guy pointed away from the water in a way where he got to stretch his arm closer to Betsy-Sue. Being close to her was the best thing he could possibly imagine. "That way!"

"I'll race you to it," she said.

"Wait, I'll meet you ou—"

But Betsy-Sue was already running out of frame.

* * *

Hey.

It's me, the narrator.

So this has all been pretty wholesome stuff so far. Puppets and excitement and love. Good dental hygiene.

I mean, there was that thing with the wrong call and the one sort of scary moment where Guy thought he might be blind, but for the most part it's been all sunshine and rainbows.

It's not going to be like that forever.

Things are about to get real.

Books don't have ratings or age restrictions like movies do, but this one would be rated PG-13 if they did.

So this is where the little kids are going to want to go read *Puppet Whale* or whatever it is human kids read.

There's some nasty stuff about to come up.

We're talking eye-wandering, smooching, and real felt-based gore. Stuff meant for *adults*. That's not even to get into the stuff that's coming up in later chapters like the use of recreational drugs, stressful workplace situations, and gambling.

Honestly, I think you'd be better if you quit being a nerd and just put the book down.

But...

If you insist on reading, you'd better know that I'm only going to warn you this one time. If you keep going, I'm going to assume it means you can handle it.

I don't want to be responsible if you can't. Books are dangerous. Especially this one. It's full of ideas and nasty themes and as you may have suspected, sharks.

Got that?

Alright...

Well...

I guess you can proceed then.

If you dare.

* * *

The ocean was much rockier than it had first appeared from the beach, but Betsy-Sue didn't seem to notice. She was staring up at something in the sky, and tilted back as she was in her two-piece, Guy found himself quite distracted by the view. His eyes were fixated on about chest-level of the puppet he hoped would soon become his fiancée.

If truth be told, he might not have been thinking about their wedding in that precise moment. He was only a puppet, after all.

He realized he was staring only when she turned to him, and he snapped his attention up. She planted a quick kiss on his lips, and he vowed not to get caught looking anywhere but her eyes. He couldn't risk ruining her flirtatious mood, after all.

This was not to say he didn't steal another couple discrete glances. But he was much quicker about it.

He may have been distracted in such a way when something bumped up against the bottom of the boat the first time. But it happened so quickly that it would be impossible to say for sure.

Betsy-Sue didn't seem worried, and Guy was all too happy to have her attention on him fully when he stopped rowing.

"Oh Guy, it's such a beautiful day for a boat ride. I'm so glad you had this idea."

She had already said something similar, but Guy didn't mind. In fact, he was pleased that he was being given another chance at his line, and he wasn't about to let romance slip through his four fingers again.

"Yeah, it's a beautiful day for a boat ride. Do you know what else is *beaut-y-ful?*"

He put as much emphasis on the last word as he could, so she knew he was being romantic.

"Uhm," Betsy-Sue looked around. "The sky?" she asked.

The blue sky and its cottony-clouds seemed almost to wrap around them on this clear day. But that wasn't what Guy had meant at all.

"Uhm. Yeah. The sky is beaut-y-ful. Do you know what else is beaut-y-ful?"

"Ahhhh," she said as if she understood. But she didn't, clearly, because not only did she keep guessing, but she had to look around for inspiration. "The ocean?"

"Yeah," Guy had to concede that point. "The ocean is beaut-y-ful. Do you know what else is beaut-y-ful?"

"Oh, flowers!" she answered quickly, getting wrapped up in what she thought was a game.

"Uh, yeah," Guy sighed, realizing she was not going to ask him what *he* thought was beautiful. "Flowers are beautiful, but what I'm getting at is you are the most beautiful thing I've ever seen."

"Oh, Guy. That's such a *beautiful* thing for you to say."

"Yeah. Ever since I met you weeks ago in front of the cinnamon bun store —"

"Oh! You were so cute in your little paper hat and your name tag."

"Yeah," he had to admit. He was letting her derail him again, but he *had* been awfully cute in his little paper hat and his name tag. It was one of the biggest perks of working at the cinnamon bun store. Well, that and carrying the scent of warm cinnamon buns home on his felt skin. And sometimes the manager wasn't there, and he could shove his whole head under the icing spout and drink the icing, which he thought tasted like melted marshmallows.

Now Guy was derailing *himself*.

"That's true," he said, trying to get back on track. "But, I guess I always wanted to ask you a question."

"What is it?"

This time the bump under the bottom of the boat was louder — so loud that Betsy-Sue looked away. Guy took the opportunity to pull the ring out of his pocket.

It was big, and sparkly, and it took up most of his palm with its glittering stones. The diamonds formed a flower petal pattern around a central, pink gem that may as well have been made specifically to match Betsy-Sue's lips. The ring may have been chosen by the grace of the claw machine, but it simply couldn't have been more perfect.

"Did you see something?" Betsy-Sue asked him.

Thump!

The sound of something hitting the boat was getting louder with each pass.

Thump!

"What was that?"

Thump!

On the final thump, the collision was so undeniable that it actually shook the boat. As Guy and Betsy-Sue were jostled in the little water vehicle, Guy felt the ring bounce right up and out of his hand.

Plop!

The mysterious presence circling beneath them was all but entirely forgotten as he struggled to comprehend the loss of the ring. The surprise. His life savings. His chance with Betsy-Sue. All of it was now sinking deeper and deeper down into the ocean.

"Ah!" He spluttered in his panic. "Ah! Ah! Ah!"

"Did you drop something?" His girlfriend asked. When she turned back to look at him, he was still gasping, open-mouthed and dumbfounded.

"Ah! Ah! Ah! Yes!"

"Well what was it?"

"Ah- ah- ah- a diamond ring!"

"A diamond ring?"

He couldn't believe he had ruined the surprise even further, on top of all the other tragedies that had befallen him in the last minute. But Betsy-Sue didn't even seem to pick up on the implication of the diamond, so much as she picked up on the urgency that expensive jewelry was now sinking into the water. The question was barely out of her mouth before she seemed determined to answer it, diving overboard to collect that ring.

She *wanted* that diamond, and Guy loved her for it. It was one of the last things he would ever love her for.

"Wait!" he called, suddenly remembering the ominous sound.

Betsy-Sue wasn't listening. She could see the sparkle of the ring fading further and further away, seeming to invite her to swim after it. Guy could see nothing from the boat.

"Where are you?" he called hopelessly.

She could neither hear him, nor answer.

The puppet shark had already set its eyes upon her.

"Betsy-Sue?" Guy called from the boat.

The shark wiggled in the water just as quickly and fluidly as if the shark were a hand and the ocean nothing more than air.

"Betsy-Sue!"

Her world went as black as if she were wearing a sleep mask the moment shark opened its mouth to reveal two rows of pointed teeth closing around her. The last thing she heard was the terrible chip-crunching sound of her own body.

Guy couldn't hear that, but he could feel the ominous music in his whole body. He looked from one side of the boat to the other in a panic. He was desperate for any sign of where his beautiful girlfriend had disappeared to.

The water had not been safe for Betsy-Sue, and the boat was not safe for Guy, for the puppet shark still circled, hungry.

Before Guy could so much as suspect what was coming, it had taken its second bite out of Guy's head. He was decapitated much like a Cheeto being snapped at the tip.

Then, there was no one left to mourn Betsy-Sue.

The puppet body stood upright, but its hands moved no more.

SRS

PRESENTS

PUPPET SHARK

THE NOVELIZATION

We Meet Our Narrator, Me, Fisherman Fred, and Our Two Young "Heroes"

You probably have some questions about this book.

Why are all the characters puppets? Was this the sort of movie that needed to be novelized? Is it okay for my children to be reading this? Who is this handsome devil of a puppet narrating?

Well, you know how I feel about answering dumb questions already, but that last one was pretty good. And I have to admit, I'm flattered.

So we'll skip over those first three, and I'll go ahead and introduce myself.

My name is Fisherman Fred. I am indeed quite a handsome puppet. I'm yellow, very human shaped (I'm quite proud of that) and with all the accessories you could want. Vest? Check. Flannel? Check. Fisherman hat? Well of course.

I am going to be your narrator through this grim tale of terror — or tail of terror, if you will. Because of the sharks. So if you have any questions... well, you can keep those to yourself, and that would be great. But if you want entertainment, with a healthy dose of shark and an even healthier dose of puppets? Then I'm your guy. Not Guy. We're not going to be talking about that particular Guy anymore.

Just like any book needs a narrator, so too do they need heroes. So now that you've met me, I figure it's time to introduce you to the "heroes" of the story.

You may have noticed that I put "heroes" in quotation marks. This is not another puppetism — a word I just coined to describe our specific mannerisms of speaking that you human readers might not be familiar with. I wish I had coined it a little earlier, so I'd had it ready to use when I first introduced the concept back in the prologue, but hey!

Nobody's perfect!

And this narrating business is real tricky when it just falls into your lap like this. It's not like I came prepared to tell a bunch of humans how one of the scariest nights in all puppet history went down.

Anyway, this part isn't about me. It's about the "heroes".

That word also isn't in quotation marks because I mean to imply that these two young boys (who you'll meet in a second) don't qualify as heroes. Absolutely they do. There is nothing more courageous than a couple of youngsters who are passionate about the art of storytelling. Especially when they have an interest in sharks.

The only issue I have with the word "hero" is that it is usually intended to refer to a character in a book who has a great journey over the course of their story. You know what I'm talking about. Like Puppet Ahab. Or Puppet Nemo. Or Quint.

These boys are heroes in the sense that they're brave, and they're more or less the main characters of the story. You can meet them and get to know them, and I wouldn't blame you in the slightest if you get invested enough to root for them when they inevitably get chased by the titular puppet shark. (You might be the kind of person who roots for the puppet shark in this scenario and while I would question that choice, I certainly wouldn't tell you to stop. That seems like your own business.)

But they're also narrators in their own right. Much as I will be telling this whole story to you, the boys will be telling smaller stories to one another. And the book will be made up of these little stories as much as it will be made up of chapters.

In a movie this would be called an "anthology" format, but that means something different in the literary world, which we are now stepping into together. I don't know if there's a word for this in books... but we're going to call it... a shortology. For short stories.

No.

A sharkology.

For short stories about *sharks*.

Because that's a word I also just now coined, you can call it another puppetism if you'd like. And with that settled, I can introduce you to the heroes/aspiring narrators of our own sharkology book; Hunter and Grayson.

Oh wait!

I completely forgot, you already met Grayson. He was the one in the camo shirt earlier. I don't remember if I mentioned that or not — but you definitely saw him. The camo doesn't work very well. He was the one who accidentally ended up on the phone call with Guy in the prologue.

Remember him?

Well, he was one of the two heroes of the story, alongside his brother, Chance.

And when you meet the brothers, which I'm deciding is right now, they were sitting in their house, getting ready for their big camping trip.

"Uhm, let's see if we have everything ready for

our camping trip," Chance said. He was a blond puppet in a red shirt, and was wearing glasses. He also had a piece of paper and a pen, which he was using more or less to take inventory. "Uhm, let's see, shirts?"

"Check," Grayson said from just behind him. He was a blond puppet in a camo shirt, which I've now established two or three times, but we'll move past it now.

"Uhm, er, pants?" Chance asked.

"Check," Grayson replied.

"Uh. Portable drill?"

Grayson didn't say anything about that one, he just slid the drill across the table. He didn't really like to talk about the drill, as acknowledging it gave the room a rather hostile vibe. It seemed like the kind of thing someone could use as a prop in a low-budget, but very compelling short horror film that their parents probably wouldn't let them watch until they were at least thirteen. He made sure the drill was in Chance's view long enough to be crossed off the list before sliding it away to the rest of their supplies.

That seemed to be good enough, because Chance moved on without further comment. "Okay. Uhm. Pajamas?"

He was happy not to be talking about the drill anymore, but he was also getting restless. "Check."

"And Whoopee cushion?"

Grayson pulled the Whoopee cushion out, almost insulted that Chance even had to ask. He would never go *anywhere* without that. "Check."

"I think we have everything."

"Check, check, check."

I probably don't have to translate that one for you, but the repetition of that last word was something done in pure excitement. It's a common thing we do as puppets, who are by nature, both repetitive and excitable. Grayson was excited — and not only about the camping trip in question, but about the ride over.

Chance and Grayson drove themselves away from the safety of their parents' house, and into the more exotic land of Shearer Park.

Now, you might be wondering at this point of the story how old these boys are. Is it common for puppet teenagers to play with Whoopee cushions? Is it normal — or in fact safe — for puppet children or pre-teens to be driving on plastic motorcycles without puppet adult supervision?

I understand why you would be curious to mildly worried about such things, but I'll tell you now as someone who knows better, that what you *should* be worried about is Shearer Park.

The ride there was totally safe, but the woods had a nasty reputation. They may have been Canada's most beautiful and puppet-friendly camping woods, but they had also been the site of several disappearances, urban legends, and strange anomalies.

Needless to say, it was no spot for two kids who were all alone.

Heck, I'm not even sure that it's safe for you to be reading about. You'd better keep your eyes out for danger too as I take you through this.

But Grayson and Chance smiled the whole drive over, and even posed in front of the Shearer Park sign if you can believe it.

"I really love camping," Chance told his brother as they started their long trek out into the woods.

"Me too," Grayson agreed.

"I really love being unsupervised."

"Me too."

This is the sort of dialogue all puppet children must surely have *before* they go missing. After a long,

long walk through the trees, and a lot of similar back and forth between the brothers, Grayson started to think along those same lines. "This place gives me the hibby-jibbies."

That's what we puppets say, instead of heebie-jeebies.

"Yeah!" Chance agreed, only he sounded too excited about it. There is a small chance he thought "hibby-jibbies" were a kind of dessert, which is what he had actually been thinking about while his brother had been talking. "The first thing I'm going to do is eat some marshmallows."

"The first thing I'm going to do is use the restroom," Grayson answered. It was easier not to get scared when he was thinking about his plans.

"I hate these dumb mosquitos," Chance said, slapping at one of the insects. They may have been too small for the human eye to see, but he could feel the itching every time one bit him.

"Yeah."

"Dumb mosquitos!" he repeated.

Grayson was reminded of a phone call earlier where he hadn't had much to say, only this time he had the added pressure of trying to impress his brother. The best he could come up with was, "Yeah."

Once they got a decent way into the woods, and after Chance had eaten a marshmallow, and then waited for his brother to use the restroom, it was time for the two of them to set up the tent.

Puppet tents were notoriously easy to set up, but then again, they sort of have to be, don't they? For puppets to be able to do it?

Another good thing about puppet tents is that they're also massive in relation to the size of a puppet. With the help of the instruction manual, one another, and mostly the wind, the two brothers took only a few minutes to set up a tent that was more or less the size of their entire living room back at home.

"Having fun?" Grayson asked as they settled in.

"Sure," Chance said uncertainly. He didn't want to be a party pooper, but so far, the trip had been a lot of work. Now it was starting to get dark and chilly — even in their tent, and Chance was wondering if the entire thing had been a bad idea.

"Hoot! Hoot!"

There was a mysterious cry from outside, and Chance nearly jumped out of his felt. "Ah! What was that?"

"Just an owl," Grayson answered.

There was no way Grayson could have been completely certain about this, but for your own peace of mind I will confirm this for you. It was indeed an owl. To be more specific, it was a puppet owl, but whenever two puppets are conversing about any sort of creature, the word puppet is very much implied as an adjective.

"You're not scared, are you?"

Chance didn't want to admit that he *had* been scared, and tried to sound cool, even as he stammered through his answer. "O-o-of course not. Owls give a hoot. They don't pollute." Nailed it, buddy. "We're perfectly safe."

But he didn't *feel* safe. And he didn't love the silence, which felt like it could be interrupted any moment by the sound of another hoot. It was the same uneasy feeling his brother had undoubtedly felt about the power drill.

"Let's just have some marshmallows," he said.

That would make him feel better.

"You'd better not eat them all," Grayson warned.

Chance spit out the massive marshmallow that

had already made its way into his mouth. "Of course not!"

"Because," his brother continued as if he had not been interrupted, "this is Lake Marsh: Home of the Great Canadian Marshmallow Shark."

Chance had been alive just as long, if not longer than Grayson, and he had never heard of such a thing in his life. "The what?"

Grayson met his eyes. He was dead serious. "The Great Canadian Marshmallow Shark. It's one of Canada's monster legends. Like Ogo Pogo, The Serpent Of Some Lake I've Never Been To. And Luguru, The Werewolf."

"Stop pulling my leg."

This was a silly thing to say, because as we all know, puppets don't have legs.

Grayson shook his head gravely, and didn't point that out. "I'm not pulling your leg. But the Great Canadian Marshmallow Shark may just chomp it off if you don't feed him marshmallows. Although, he does prefer hands."

If he preferred legs, he'd go hungry a lot, I imagine.

"You're crazy," Chance told him, though more than anything he hoped Grayson was just lying. "Sharks don't live in this lake. It's a freshwater lake, and besides, sharks don't eat marshmallows."

"Alright," Grayson shrugged. "If you say so."

It was always most suspicious when his brother just agreed, and Chance really didn't want to have to deal with the silence again. "Alright, alright," he said. "You can tell your story, but I am eating another marshmallow."

"All I know," Grayson said, "is that the story goes back to ancient times. The 1960's."

The Origin of The Great Canadian Marshmallow Shark
(as told by Grayson, as told by me, Fisherman Fred)

It all started a long time ago, on a night just like this. On this very spot...

There were two hippies out on the beach. They were happy-go-lucky, freedom-loving puppets who believed in world peace and minimal government interference when it came to certain recreational activities. They were enjoying one another's company under a sunset sky of green and orange that was almost as psychedelic as their souls.

"I love these brownies," said the blonde, girl puppet as she munched down on the rest of the baked goods. "I baked them, and they baked me, thanks to the secret ingredient."

Brett nodded along, staring off into the distance. It was hard to focus on anything else because he too was feeling pretty baked. He might not have had any of his girlfriend's brownies, but he'd had plenty of the secret ingredient.

"Dude!" she exclaimed, a thought suddenly coming to her. "Do you ever think that cannabis will be legal in Canada?"

Whoops, there goes the secret I guess.

"Not in our lifetime, Honeypie."

"Oh well," she sighed. She hoped that kids reading about her generations later might live in a world where cannabis was appreciated more for it's relaxing and medicinal qualities. (If she had known why kids would still be reading about her generations later, she might have had other concerns.) "Live for today."

This is always good advice, kids, but it was especially good advice for Honeypie, and especially on that particular day.

They were both silent for awhile as they drank in the beautiful colors of the natural world. It was Honeypie who eventually broke that silence. "I love communing with nature." There hadn't been much communing on Brett's end. He had been having a more passive appreciation for the beach, a place where it was most acceptable to wear his cool vest that exposed the yellow felt of his chest. But he liked that Honeypie was getting something more meaningful out of the beach trip. She was a very profound person, and he loved that about her. Plus, she had a real way with words. "It's so... natural."

He didn't have anything to say that could top that, even when he looked out over the water for inspiration. It was blue, and there were little waves rippling in the otherwise calm waters. But that didn't move him much, so he just said what was on his mind. "It's really quiet up here. I'm surprised there aren't more campers."

"I'm not complaining," Honeypie said. "I like being able to be free. And to be me."

"How about some groovy music?" he asked, holding up his guitar.

Brett had always been better with chords than with words. He was so good with his unplugged electric guitar in fact, that he was able to make it sound more like an entire synth band, complete with drums and everything. Honeypie gasped in excitement to hear him play.

She danced along to his groovy beats, and for a little while the sky and sand seemed to blend together like liquid paints.

"Hey," Brett asked when his attention was pulled from the music by a low rumble in his stomach. He wasn't ready to end the party just yet, but he could most definitely go for a snack. "You got any more of them special brownies?"

Honeypie looked down solemnly. "No. But we've got a bunch of marshmallows."

It took her a minute to actually produce any marshmallows, and she only showed him one. When she presented it to him, it was skewered on a large stick, and she looked deadly serious about it.

"Honeypie, what is it?"

"I've got an idea. How about we go for a midnight swim?"

Brett shook his head, suddenly feeling quite a bit more serious as well. "I'm not sure that's a good idea."

"It's the grooviest idea!"

Back in those days, it was very hard for any self-respecting hippy puppet to argue once the word groovy had been thrown around, but Brett's silence on the matter spoke volumes.

"Come on, party pooper," Honeypie told him. "First one in the water gets the marshmallow!"

With that she took off down the beach.

"Honeypie, wait!" When she didn't wait, he sighed. "Ugh. I'd better go after her."

The shore hadn't seemed too far away, but it felt like a long time before he caught up to Honeypie. He was surprised when he got there and found her still standing by the lake.

"You're not in the water yet?"

"No. I wanted to drink in all this glorious nature."

"Yeah," he was so relieved. "It's probably too cold anyway. We should go back."

"No, wait!" Honeypie sounded so excited. "I think I see something in the lake!"

The water looked just as calm up close as it had from a distance. Brett didn't see anything personally, but even if he had, he didn't understand why it should be a surprise. "Of course you do. There's tadpoles and fish—"

"Oh! I love fish!" Brett had forgotten just how easily Honeypie could get excited about nature's creatures. "I want to see the fish! Here fishy fishy fishy fishy! I don't have any worms, but uh," her eyes fell on what she did have, "I have marshmallows."

Brett didn't like to correct her, but sometimes he just couldn't help it. The last thing he wanted was for her to get disappointed after getting her hopes up. "Fish don't eat marshmallows."

Honeypie didn't like that much at all. "You just want them all for yourself."

Brett didn't have a response to that. He did want them all to himself, and it was clear she didn't want to see reason.

"Here, fishy fishy fishy!"

Brett looked out at the blue vastness of the unchanging water for as long as he had the patience for: nearly six seconds. "I'm tired and you're wasted. Time to go."

But just as he was turning away, he heard Honeypie gasp. When he looked back over at the water, even he had to admit that the sight was beautiful.

The puppet shark!

It was leaping out of the air, making a perfect arc before splashing back into the lake water.

"Did you see that?" Honeypie demanded.

"Was that a shark?" We know it was actually a puppet shark, but I will take this further opportunity to remind you that the 'puppet' here is implied. "That's impossible!"

Honeypie, who was literally jumping for joy at the sight, was a lot less worried about what was and was not possible. She was just excited to be having such an experience. "A shark! A shark! That was — that has to be my spirit animal!"

This is something that probably wouldn't have flown in modern day Canada. Kids these days are a lot more socially aware than they were in ancient times. A big part of being open-minded and peace-loving is knowing that terms like "spirit animal" are a type of cultural appropriation.

But in Honeypie's defense here, she is a puppet, and this was before puppets were ready to have that sort of open dialogue about the mistreatment of indigenous puppets. I doubt you're ready to have that sort of conversation from this book in particular, so we're just going to move right along from her ignorant remark to Brett's poor response.

"You need to be spirited away from here, is what I think."

He laughed a little at his own joke, which is never cool.

"No!" Honeypie insisted. "I want to see the shark!"

The shark, it seemed, was also eager to be seen. It was swimming excitedly in preparation for another leap. Neither it, nor Brett, was prepared for Honeypie to start singing.

> *"Oh my Shark-y*
> *Little Shark-y*
> *Oh my darling,*
> *Sharky Dear.*
>
> *Won't you come up*
> *For marshmallows*
> *'Cause I have them*
> *All right here."*

She really did have the marshmallows — at least the one she had brought over with her to the edge of the water. And the shark seemed to be responding because she could feel the ripples in the water as the shark prepared to leap once more. Its fin could be seen breaking through the waves as he got closer.

Even Brett was impressed. "Way out. Totally way, way out."

The puppet shark made another bold leap from the water, taking a big bite from the offered marshmallow before landing again.

Honeypie gasped in delight. "See? I told you he liked marshmallows."

The puppet shark leapt again, this time straight at Honeypie. He didn't make scenic arc over the horizon or soar majestically overhead to steal another bite of marshmallow. The shark came straight at her, and Honeypie's vision went as red as what her puppet blood might have looked like if puppets had blood.

What they did have was bones.

By the time the shark was in the water once more, Brett could see for himself that puppets had bones because Honeypie's arm bone was sticking straight out of her shoulder felt — where just a minute ago there had been a limb.

"Oh, spirit animal!" she called. It's this next line

for which her character should truly be judged though, for it proves her intentions were better than her verbalization of them. As she waved her arm — or lack thereof — she cried out to the puppet shark. "I forgive you!"

She did.

And she continued loudly forgiving him.

"I learned your great lesson! It's not nice to fool with Mother Nature! Ahhhh!"

That last bit was the fading, whispering sound she made as she collapsed backwards into the sand.

I will leave it to our readers individually to decide whether or not the puppet shark was actually trying to teach a lesson. I have my own opinions about this, of course, but I'm not about to engage in another lesson in puppet philosophy or puppet shark ethics. I'd much rather tell you how cool the puppet shark looked zooming around under the water with Honeypie's arm in its mouth proudly. It was not unlike how a dog might hold a prized stick, only terrifying.

"Honeypie!" Brett called when the shock of what he was seeing wore off a little. (He couldn't see that bit about the shark underwater, that was just a little detail I included for the audience.) His beloved Honeypie was on the ground with her arm bone out. "No!"

When he saw the fin approaching he was quick to take action, and grateful he had thought to bring along the rest of the marshmallows.

"Here!" he shouted, tossing a handful at the water.

The puppet shark grabbed a marshmallow that was almost as big as his entire body and shook it in ravenous victory.

"Take all the marshmallows!" Brett cried as he lamented still, hardly caring if the shark was sated or not. "Dumb shark! Why? Nature, we trusted you!"

When he was done screaming, and it did not seem like the shark would be surfacing for him next, he rushed to scoop up what was left of Honeypie.

"Oh god!" He didn't know if he was more upset by the fin on the horizon or how weightless and floppy Honeypie now felt in his arms. "No! Get away from us you dumb shark! Honeypie, stay with me."

She opened her mouth and in response sang a slow, sad song.

> *"Oh my shark-y*
> *Little shark-y*
> *All my marsh-*
> *Mallows you took*
>
> *We are joined now*
> *Bound forever*
> *Like the croc*
> *And Captain Hook."*

Brett let out the saddest sound, perhaps that any puppet had ever made. It was a wail and a sob, and the end of his groovy vibe forever.

The puppet shark swam on.

Brett's life was spared, but only at the cost of his love and also all of his marshmallows.

A Very Stinky Secret

"And that's the origin of the Great Canadian Marshmallow Shark," Grayson concluded.

"What do you call shark doodoo?" Chance asked. "'Cause you're full of it!"

Grayson didn't think that was a particularly scathing insult. "I prefer to be full of marshmallows. And so does the shark! So you'd better save some for him."

"You're just trying to scare me," Chance said, and he hoped it was true. He'd already eaten most of the marshmallows, and his brother's story was ambiguous about how many he'd actually need to fend off a shark.

"Hoot!" cried the owl, and that didn't make him feel any better. But he wasn't having it anymore.

"Look," he said pointedly. "I've had enough. I'm not scared, and I don't believe a word of your dopey story."

"Hmmm," said Grayson, like it didn't really matter to him. "I just tell them how I see them."

He hoped his persistence would make Chance curious again, but his brother only turned away.

"Where are you going?" he asked.

"Hoot!" cried the owl again.

By the time Grayson got over to the flap of the tent where Chance was sitting, he found him just staring off into space. Grayson tapped him on the shoulder repeatedly, trying to reclaim his attention.

"Yeah, Grayson?"

"Can I tell you a secret?"

"Sure!"

Grayson leaned in close and put his hand over his mouth before whispering so low that even I, the narrator, couldn't hear his words. By the time he pulled away, Chance's jaw was hanging wide open in shock. He had his hand over his mouth as well.

"What?" Grayson asked, for this was clearly not the reaction he was expecting from whatever mysterious thing he said. "What? You didn't like my secret?"

Chance looked at him seriously. "Grayson. Have you ever heard the saying that it's not what you said, it's how you say it?"

"Yeah."

"Let's just say that your secret stunk."

Grayson thought about that hard before admitting defeat. "I don't get it."

"Your breath, Grayson. What have you been eating?"

He had to think about it. Grayson had never exactly been as snack-minded as his brother. "I dunno. I had some marshmallows earlier."

"Really?" Chance had expected the answer to be something a lot worse than that, like brussels sprouts or fish. "Did you brush your teeth this morning?"

"Yeah," he answered.

"Did you floss?"

"Well. Sort of?"

That answer puzzled Chance. It was even more

exasperating than a 'no' would have been. "How do you 'sort of' floss?"

"Well... well I sort of look at the floss." Grayson shifted uncomfortably at his brother's interrogation. "I sort of pick it up. And I sort of ... put it back in the drawer.

Chance was absolutely scandalized at this. "Grayson. You need to floss. Every day."

Grayson didn't much like being told how to behave from his brother. "Says who?"

"Says the dentist. And says Mom. And Dad. Now says me."

Grayson *especially* didn't like that Chance was now considering himself an authority figure on the same level of Dad, Mom, and the dentist. Luckily for Grayson, Chance was easier to argue with than any of those very serious adults.

"Mmm, but who else?" he asked.

Chance got irritated right away and lost his cool. "I can't believe it! You need to start flossing!"

"Now you *do* sound like the dentist," Grayson pointed out. This *was* a scathing insult, far worse than the one Chance had thrown his way earlier about shark doodoo. That one was hypothetical, and metaphorical, and maybe a bit more called for. But this one *hurt*. Who wants to go camping with someone who sounds like a dentist?

"How do you think *he* feels?" Chance demanded. "Do you think he enjoys telling people to floss all the time? Do you think he likes looking into the witch's cauldron of the mouth every nine months?"

Grayson hadn't expected Chance to take this so personally, or to be attacked in kind. "Now you're just being rude."

Chance's voice softened. "Sorry, Grayson. I didn't mean to be."

Wouldn't it be better if all brothers acted like this? It's in puppet nature to get overexcited and snap and sometimes make mean comments about the dentist, but I think human puppets would fare better if they learned to get along like these two.

"That's okay. Apology accepted."

The easier it is for a person to see their mistakes and sincerely apologize, the easier it is to forgive them.

Chance smiled. "Hey, this reminds me of a story."

"Oh, I love stories!"

"This one has a dentist in it!"

"Okay, Chance, I get it."

"The dentist who almost gave up!"

"*I* give up." Grayson really did look like he was about to give up, but Chance knew just exactly how to bring him back.

"But this story has a *shark*."

A quick tip for any of the readers who would like to become storytellers of their own some day. The one thing that can make any story better is always, without fail, a shark. If you want to get someone to listen to your story or read your book or even watch your movie, the best possible decision you can make is to advertise the shark in it.

Likewise, if you're trying to teach an important lesson to your child or sibling or really smelly friend, the best thing you can do is to tell them that lesson in a way that involves sharks.

It worked like a charm, and Grayson smiled wide. "I'm in."

"Great, here we go."

The Peculiar Patient of Dr. Dental

(as told by Chance, as told by me, Fisherman Fred)

Many years ago, there was a dentist named Dr. Dental. He was a kind man with a convenient last name. He enjoyed his patients, his job, and his fish…

"Where's the shark?" Grayson interrupted. "There's no way it's gonna fit in a fish tank."

"Give it a moment," Chance told him. "We haven't gotten there yet."

"Sorry."

"Can I continue?"

"Please do."

"Thank you."

"You're welcome."

And Chance continued…

One thing he did not like though, was constantly telling his patients to floss. He was staring into the gaping mouth of one such patient, poking around with what was definitely a real dental tool and not something sculptors use for clay.

"Looks good," he said in his warm, deep voice. It

was one of his best qualities, for it matched his personality quite well and often came in handy when it was time to reassure his patients. "Now, I did notice some bleeding along the gum line. You really should remember to floss."

"Ahhhh uh ahh oh ah," said the patient, because they had to keep their mouth open while he worked.

"Do you remember me telling you to do that the last time you were here?" he prompted, because dentists could never seem to remember that they were the ones keeping the patients' mouths open. That seems awfully silly, since it's their rule, but this is something that is unfortunately same in both the puppet and human worlds.

"Ah oh ah hm ah!" The patient tried again, but their words were equally unintelligible.

"Remember to floss."

"Ah ha eh ah ahh ah ah-a-a-eh."

They were pretty triumphant as they concluded that attempt, thinking they'd gotten something across. Dennis the dentist pulled his tools and puppet fingers from their mouth, looking as though he had just understood something really serious.

"See? Yeah. See ... yeah." Dr. Dental almost sounded like he was the one trying to talk with his mouth open. His words were slow and his expression was vacant as he struggled with an idea that had just come to him. After a moment of muttering he found the courage to say what was on his mind. "See ya!"

He waved to the patient and headed out of the office, which was certainly an odd and abrupt way to conclude a scheduled visit.

"See ya!" he called to his receptionist as he headed to the front door.

"But Dr. Dental! Your 11:00 appointment's here to see you."

"See you," he said. And then, just in case she missed his point, he said it one more time. "See ya!"

She watched, open-mouthed and wide-eyed as he left...

"So what did he do?" Grayson interrupted, and here I have another quick tip for the audience.

While it's never polite to interrupt a storyteller mid story, it's better to interrupt with an excited question like this than it is to interrupt with a complaint or random observation.

Earlier, Chance was annoyed that Grayson was interrupting the story to point out that there were no sharks. He knew that the shark was still coming, and was irritated that his brother didn't trust him to include a shark. But when interrupted the second time, he knew it was because his brother was invested in the story, and worried about the fate of the kind-hearted but tired Dr. Dennis Dental. This question gave him something to play off of, and it made the story more engaging and fun.

"Remember when I said he loved his fish?"

"Yeah."

"Well, his fish were the only thing that brought him peace. So he thought, what better place to relax than the beach?"

"Makes sense."

As he looked out into the ocean, he still did not feel relaxed. The beach was so very noisy, and all he could think of was all those people along the shore not flossing.

His fish in the office were the only things that

calmed him down. So the dentist was thinking that if the small fish in his office kept him calm then…

"Then a big fish would calm him down even more!"

"Exactly."

"So off he went to catch the biggest fish he could think of — a shark!"

He had a Hawaiian T-shirt on right over his dentist uniform as he sat on the boat with his fishing rod. Dr. Dental considered himself somewhat of a great fisherman, and had caught all of his office fish himself. He didn't see why he couldn't also catch the shark for himself too.

"What a beautiful day!" he said. "The sun is shining. The ocean is calm and steady. Just me and my best chum."

Now, when he said chum, it's important to mention that he meant the sort of chum you might use to catch a shark. In some parts of the human world, I understand, that chum can also mean friend, so I wanted to clarify. I don't want you getting the wrong idea about Dr. Dental when I tell you he was throwing chopped up bits of his chum over the side of his boat.

"Now we wait."

A shark was swimming by at this exact same time, and he was enjoying his day without a care in the world.

"What a beautiful day," the shark said. "I wonder what kind of excitement the day will bring."

He didn't have to wait long to find out. No sooner had he said those words than a delicious piece of chum fell right into his mouth. He swallowed it with a big gulp and was thrilled! It tasted great!

And there was another one!

And another one!

He followed the trail of chum, gobbling up each piece as he got closer to the surface.

"Wow! What a fantastic treat to come across. I wonder if I follow the food, where does it go?"

He was already following the food, so he kept going.

"I bet there's one of those pointy hook things up there. I don't trust this." But he kept going anyway. Before you judge him, I'd implore you to ask yourself whether or not you'd have the ability to resist following a trail of tasty treats. "No sir."

He kept swimming after the trail. It just tasted so good.

When he got to the last piece of chum, he could see that it was, as he had suspected all along, attached to one of those pointy hook things.

"There it is!" he exclaimed. Even though he was disappointed, it made him feel awfully smart to be right. "The pointy hook."

That wasn't good. But he didn't leave right away either.

"Hmmm," he said as he swallowed the penultimate piece of chum, "that seems to be the last morsel." He watched the pointy hook swing back and forth in the water. "Except this one."

The little shark couldn't help but swim even closer to the last bit of food. It smelled so very good, and being a shark, he was plenty hungry for it. "I wonder if I should take it."

Then the puppet shark followed the pointy thing with his eyes, to where the line was connected to something above the water. "Maybe I should ask the owner."

"Whoa!" shouted Dr. Dental, for he felt the powerful currents rocking the boat and even shaking his fishing pole as the shark ascended. "This must be a big one! You hear that, shark?"

But when there was no immediate answer, he didn't let himself get too discouraged. "Ah, what do you know anyway?" he asked, and turned his attention back to the line. "She's almost there! I can feel it!"

...

...

...

"Is that it?" Grayson demanded.

"Is what it?" Chance asked. This time he was annoyed again, because this was not one of the parts of the story where he welcomed any kind of interruption.

"Aren't they going to say anything?"

"Give it a moment!" Chance said. "This is for dramatic effect."

"Ahhhh. Fancy."

"Right?" Chance asked. That was exactly the word he would have used as well, and he went from being irritated to being awfully proud of himself.

He was allowed to finish his dramatic pause in mutual silence.

...

...

...

The shark poked its head up out of the water and

onto the side of the boat. Dr. Dental let out a little "eek!"

Even though he had been expecting a shark, he'd been prepared to reel one in on his fishing line, not see one pop up randomly over the side to see him.

"Do you mind?" the shark asked.

"Sorry," Dr. Dental said, even though he was the one who had been startled. "I didn't mean to offend."

"I didn't mean that," the shark corrected, for he realized how the question could have been misinterpreted. "I mean, do you mind if I have this?" He nodded his shark head toward the last piece of chum.

"What, the hook?"

"No, no. Not the hook. What's on the hook."

"Well," Dr. Dental hesitated. "If you eat what's on the hook, then I win."

The shark was confused. "Win what?"

"Win you."

"Ahhh," said the shark, though he still didn't fully understand. He let out a large breath as he tried to buy time and the dentist shook a little.

"Fwaaah!"

The shark was pretty proficient in puppet speak, but had never heard that word before. "What did you say?"

"I said 'fwaaah!'"

"Meaning?"

"Your breath is… is… fwaaah!"

"Is that another word for stinky?" asked the shark, who I think was being pretty reasonable for an apex predator who was just insulted by a dentist who had also just threatened to win him.

"No, no no no. Stink is downright unpleasant. Peculiar. Downright awful. This? This has no words. It's just… it's… it's fwaaah!"

"You know what is really sad?" the shark asked.

"What's that?"

"I've had hurtful things said like that to me before. It's not my fault."

"I didn't mean to hurt your feelings," Dr. Dental said. The shark didn't know he was in a very breath-based business after all, and the criticism had been rather harsh now that he stopped to think about it.

"That's okay," said the shark. "I've had this affliction for quite some time. I've tried just about everything, but no luck. I just wish there was someone who could help me."

Dr. Dental had an idea. "Hey! Wait a second! I could have a look."

"You can?"

"Absolutely! I was so wrapped up being a fisherman that I completely forgot that I'm also a dentist."

"You're kidding!" the shark exclaimed, because it simply felt like too large of a coincidence for him to believe.

"Nope! For real!"

"That would be great if you don't mind!"

Dr. Dental had never seen a shark look so excited to run into a dentist. "It would be no bother at all! Let me get my stuff."

For some reason, the dentist was calm at this moment. He took a deep breath.

The doctor was all set up to see where the fwaaah! smell was coming from

"I have my kit, my underwater mask, and my nose plug."

The shark was flattered that the doctor's underwater mask had cartoon sharks over the eyes. It made him feel like a celebrity, and that feeling of flattery went a long way to heal the hurt of knowing a nose plug would required.

"My patient! Are you ready?"

"I'm ready!"

"Open wide!"

So he did.

"'Ow's the nose plug holding up doc?" He asked, and Dr. Dental was awfully impressed that he could more or less understand the shark's words — even when the shark was holding his mouth open. He had to be very still, because his two rows of pointed teeth were so sharp, and the dentist had to reach his arm right in.

"So far so good."

"'Oo see anything?"

"Aside from a bunch of sharp teeth, nothing yet."

He felt around the teeth with his very real dentist tools, working more carefully than he ever had in his whole life. "Hey," he asked his peculiar patient. "I have a question for you."

"Shoot!"

"Are you experiencing any pain anywhere? You have a very big mouth, no offense."

"'One taken."

"So, uh, any pain?"

"Now that you mention it, I've had a bit of dull pain towards 'de back."

"Your back?"

"'De back! On the left!"

"Sounds good," Dr. Dental said, reaching his hand in further and gently prodding the teeth he felt may be a problem. "Nope. Nope."

"'Oo you see anything yet, Doc?"

"Not yet! Nope. Nope. Nope. Wait a second!" A terrible thought struck him when he saw a large mass wedged between two of his patient's sharp teeth.

"Doc?"

"Have you eaten any cheese lately?"

"Cheese? Not for awhile."

"How long ago?"

The shark had to think about it, which was never a good sign. "It's been years!" And that confirmed it! "Someone put it on a shiny hook. I just assumed it was meat, so I ate it."

Dr. Dental didn't care why he had eaten it. "I think I found your problem, then. You have a piece of cheese stuck between your teeth.

"That is so strange. I mean. I brush er'y day."

"But," he hated to ask. He didn't want to ask. He couldn't ask. Not again. "Do you... do... do you..."

"Doc, you okay?"

"Do! You! Floss!"

"Floss?" asked the shark. "Well. Not every day. But most of the time."

Well, Dr. Dental had heard that before. "When was, you say, the last time you flossed?"

"Honestly?" sighed the smelly shark.

"Please!" begged Dr. Dental.

"You sure?"

"I am!"

"Alright then..."

"Let me have it," he groaned, already sure of what he would hear.

"Never."

Dr. Dental expected to lose it. He expected to be filled with the same rage that had caused him to storm out of his office earlier that same morning.

But it didn't come.

He was working on the teeth of a shark, and that reminded him so much of his fish that he felt okay. "You know what?"

"What?"

"I knew that."

It had been rather obvious to him, as it was his job

to spot that sort of thing. And hearing it really wasn't as terrible as he had thought it would be.

"So what do we do?"

It made the dentist feel good to have a patient so eager to take the next steps with his tooth care. He was fixing a big problem — and for a big fish no less! "Let me see," he said, as he went back in with his hand.

"You got this, Doc!"

The pointy teeth grazed along Dr. Dental's arm. "Shush!" He ordered. "No talking, please. I don't want to get bit."

The dentist has an idea.

"What was he up to?" Grayson asked.

"The doctor was looking for something to help him get in between the teeth," Chance answered.

"He was going between the teeth?" Grayson asked, incredulous. He would *never* want to go between a shark's teeth. "Scary."

"He was looking for something to *clean* in between the teeth, silly."

"Ohhh."

So the dentist ran back to the tooth with the cheese stuck in it as fast as he could. "Ah-ha! My fishing line!" He wielded the large string between his two hands; the most effective weapon of his trade. "Now, open wide Mr. Shark."

Mr. Shark opened very wide and the dentist muttered to himself as he work. "Uh-huh. Okay. This is good. Yeah. Yeah. That's good."

The dentist started working on the teeth. He was

moving the fishing line back and forth, back and forth until finally…

"It's good! Yes!" The cheese was gone! "Success!"

"Awesome! Thanks, Doc."

"If you do mind, no talking, please."

For the doctor still had his hands in the shark's mouth, and he was determined to finish flossing all of the many, many teeth.

It took a long time, but it was worth it. By the end his patient looked — and smelled — much better.

"Let me see. Hey, I — I've never felt more alive!" Dennis exclaimed.

"You know what, Doc? That really worked. I feel sooo much better."

"Well you should! There was so much schmutz stuck between your teeth — and you have a lot of teeth!"

"How's the breath doing? Sorry, the 'fwaaah!'" He breathed out heavily as he spoke so the doctor could smell his breath, and Dr. Dental sat up a little straighter as a result.

"Strong," he admitted, "but smells wonderful." He paused. "You know what?"

"What?"

"Thank you."

"Thank me? For what?"

The dentist went on to explain that he didn't feel stressed anymore, while the shark frolicked some in the water to celebrate. "I've never felt more relaxed. This is wonderful."

"You've got this, Doc."

"I mean, I tried those self help books, but they did nothing. Ah!"

He was happy again. He even didn't mind the word floss, and that was a big deal.

"But what happened next?"
"Well…"

The doctor headed back to his office, well-rested, and ready to work. He understood that sometimes people didn't floss, and that's okay. Sometimes, people need to remind them to. And that's okay too. There might even be those who never heard of flossing before.

"Is that okay?" Grayson asked.
"Yep!" Chance answered. "That's okay too!"

A Guest Appearance from Your Narrator, me, Fisherman Fred

"Hoot!" cried the owl, who clearly wanted another shark story. It was getting later in the night and the boys were toasting marshmallows right there in the tent.

"Pass me another marshmallow, please," Grayson asked.

"Okay," Chance answered as he reached for another marshmallow. Before he could reach it, who just happened to wander into the tent but me — Fisherman Fred?

You didn't really think they'd just let *anyone* narrate a story as important as *Puppet Shark*, did you? Of course they wouldn't. They needed a real puppet man, someone with experience. Someone who was *there*.

And there I was.

With my normal, yellow, human puppet felt, and my bushy mustache, and my even bushier eyebrows.

"Hello there, kids."

"Hi," Grayson said as he turned to look over at me.

"Hey, Fisherman Fred. How're you doing?" Chance asked.

I didn't answer him, because I didn't think the story should be about me, you understand. At this point in the tragic evening I didn't even realize the boys were *in* a story. I was more worried about finding the two young puppets all alone in Shearer Park, unsupervised, with a fire in their tent.

So instead I asked, "What are you guys doing out here?"

"Oh," Chance said, "we're just out here for a nice camping trip."

"Yep," Grayson confirmed. "Eating marshmallows. What are you doing here?"

"Oh, just taking in some nighttime fishing. I just wanted to make sure you guys were okay. You know, with all the people that go missing around these here parts. Anyway, have a good night."

Now.

I've given you a couple tips and tricks of the trade already in this book. How to listen better. How to tell a story better. How to apologize, and all that. Now I'm going to teach you something else. I'm going to teach you something about children.

If you want to tell a child to be cautious, you can't say it like a warning. Adult puppets are always telling youngsters what to do, and what not to do, and they learn to tune it out.

So if you do find yourself in a situation where you need to warn some kids — and you need them to actually *listen* to it — you've got to make them think it's their own idea to listen.

Do you need an example of this?

Earlier in this book, *I* warned *you* there was some real scary stuff and that you'd better stop reading if you didn't want to get scared. Didn't I? But did you listen?

No.

And don't try to deny it. I know you didn't listen and set the book down, because you're still here reading the dang thing. You may be a little older than the puppets I came across in their tent in the woods of Shearer Park that night, but the concept holds true. You made your own decisions and I hope you can bear the consequences of them as this story unravels.

The kids though, I felt like there was a shot for them still. I really wanted to spook them back to safety.

So I turned myself around and made it look like I was ready to march right on out of that tent.

And you know what? It worked like a charm.

"Whaa—?" Chance asked.

"Yeah, wait, what?" Grayson demanded.

"Oh, yeah," I said, playing it up like the whole thing was an afterthought and not planned. "Folks are always disappearing. But you don't have to worry," I said, knowing full well that's the thing you can say that will make a puppet worry most, "I'm close by."

"Whoa, whoa, whoa, what do you mean missing people?"

I turned back around to look at the two, wide-eyed little puppet children. I knew I had the pair of them, hook, line and sinker, if you'll pardon this old fisherman his fishing expressions. "Oh, you know. We got people going missing from their tent."

Chance gasped.

It was working, so I kept working it.

"We got people disappearing from their boats. We even have a whole independent film crew that went missing once. But you don't have to worry."

Both kids *looked* worried.

"Say what?" Chance asked, just as his brother was asking, "Huh?"

There's a strong shot that if Chance had brought up the independent film crew, Grayson would not have wanted to hear it. It sounds like the sort of story a kid would make up to get back at his brother for spooking him about The Great Canadian Marshmallow Shark earlier in the night.

But I told them, and I might as well get this part out of the way and tell you now too, that this was not a made up story at all. This here is a real one.

"Tell us that story!" Chance insisted.

"Yeah!" Grayson urged.

"Ohhh…" I pretended that I didn't want to tell them. I pretended that was the last thing I could ever want. "You don't want to hear about that one."

"Yeah, tell us a story!"

I already showed you folks at home my hand. I won't try to talk you into or out of flipping forward to that next chapter. I won't warn you about all the fights that will follow. From here on out, I'll only tell you how it happened once I got onto the scene.

"Well," I began, "it all started like this…"

An Educational Tale About How Not to Make a Shark Movie

Duncan was the most muscular puppet that I think anyone had ever seen. He had felt tires bulging out of what would otherwise be scrawny puppet arms — which all the rest of us seem to have.

They were his defining feature, and they made him look absolutely fantastic on the handheld camera of the independent crew. He looked especially incredible when he wore his black tank top, which made him look real tough.

"Hey man," said the director, who was also the cinematographer, who was also the writer and editor. What with the film crew being independent, he still had to fill multiple roles in the studio to get things done. He wanted Duncan talking to him so he could check the sound as well — which technically made him the sound guy puppet in addition to everything else.

"Hey, dude," Duncan answered.

"How's it going?"

"Good."

Duncan was not a man of many words, it would seem, just a man of many muscles.

"You all ready to film?"

"You bet!"

That was a short answer too, but the back and forth gave the director a decent enough concept of the sound quality that he felt comfortable enough continuing.

"Well, we're just waiting for Christine, but she'll be here any second now."

"Cool."

As if on cue, Christine came walking up. She was in costume already, makeup done, her red hair really popping on camera. "There she is!'

"Hi!"

"Hey, so, you ready to go make some shark movie?"

Now, you may already be seeing the problem. He said 'some' shark movie. Like he wasn't even interested in the sharks. Like it didn't matter what shark movie they were making.

If I can give you a piece of advice (and we know from experience that I can and will do just that) it's that you've got to do things in life you're passionate about. Like me, and how I love nighttime fishing.

If I can give you a second piece of advice, which again, I will, it's that you can't ever be tired of shark stories. If you're done with sharks, well then what even is the point in life?

So this director, who gets to make shark movies every day, just didn't care about them anymore. I don't know if I could even think of anything sadder than that.

But I digress.

"Yeah, sure," Christine said.

"Okay," Duncan added.

"Great. We'll just go walk through the forest here."

That got Duncan talking. More specifically, it got

Duncan complaining. "Why do we always have to film in the forest?"

"Like, there are always like, a million mosquitos," Christine added.

"I dunno. Uh, that's just something that people expect from shark movies now. There's always people walking through the forest for some reason."

"Mmmkay," said Duncan, like he had used up all his words.

"Let's do that!" the director said, like it was an idea he had just come up with and was excited to try, and not something the script had said to do all along.

"Okay," Christine said.

She was a real team player, Christine. If Duncan was on board, she was usually on board as well.

So the three puppets started off on what would be their very last long trek through the woods. And the director made sure to get every last bit of it on film.

Shots of the trees.

Shots of Duncan's head.

Clips of Christine's hair.

Times where he walked close behind them. Bits where the actors walked toward the camera.

Everything.

"We have been walking for awhile," Christine huffed.

"Yeah," the director said matter-of-factly. "Well this is a shark movie. For some reason all these shark movies have people-walking-through-the-forest montages. Uh. I don't know why, they just seem to go on forever."

"If you say so," Christine said, but she didn't sound so sure.

The crazy thing about this is that the director wasn't wrong. He may have been misguided about his career path and his lack of enthusiasm for what was objectively the coolest job in the world, but he was right about this. People walking through the woods is sort of a trope in shark movies nowadays, isn't it? I mean, I can think of four I've seen that have people walking through a bunch of trees — and that's just off the top of my head.

Oh!

Five, actually, if you want to count the moon as a forest. Uh, I'm not sure why you would want to, but if you did, I couldn't stop you. And I'd have a fifth great movie to recommend.

Anyway, the film crew.

Even Duncan was breathing heavily, despite how fit he was.

"Come on," said the director, trying to rally the others. "Let's give the people what they expect."

So there was more walking.

More shots of trees.

Plenty of panting.

"Again?" demanded Duncan, when the director urged them forward. This was the most labor intensive shark movie he had ever shot in the woods.

"Come on guys," he urged his actors.

"Yeah," said Christine again when they were on the trail again. "This amount of walking seems ridiculous."

"Yeah," Duncan agreed. "It's a little excessive."

A big word from Duncan, the director thought, but he didn't say so. "Don't sweat it," he said instead to his puppets, who were quite literally sweating. (Panting is the same thing as sweating for us puppets — we're like dogs! We don't have sweat glands, but we do funnily enough have this expression.) "This is a shark movie. Besides, we're almost there anyway."

"Okay."

"Okay, good."

"That's way too much walking," Grayson chimed in. "Do people feel ripped off by all that padding?"

"Yes," I answered honestly. "Every time."

I didn't explain to the children how art works under late-stage capitalism. People like ninety minute movies to get their money's worth, and so studios try to pressure directors to make their movie long enough to burn onto a disk and pack with extras so they can put a decent price tag on it. Then directors have to pad out their art by anywhere from twenty to forty minutes depending on what the idea was to begin with.

So then the audience gets lots of shots of things like people hiking for several minutes in a shark movie.

It's the same with books. Writers, and even narrators such as myself, we have to meet certain word count goals to get our books printed. Which, incidentally, is how you get a puppet narrator rambling for three paragraphs about the effects of capitalism on art. But I think we're getting back on track with the word count quota now.

Let me check.

Yeah, we're good.

Anyway, I didn't say that to the children, because not only is it more padding, it's sort of a bummer to think about. They're too young to be as bitter as I am, working puppet that I am. Heck, I'm too excited about sharks to linger on it any longer myself. So let's do what I did in the moment, and just get back to the story.

"Okay guys," the director said. "So here's what you're gonna do, alright? So you're gonna wrestle around a little bit and uh, you know, you're going to throw her in the water and then uh, you know, a shark's gonna come up. And he's gonna eat you."

"Okay," Christine said. All of that sounded pretty standard. "How far do we go down?"

"I dunno. Just stay up to your knees or something? I don't want you guys to get too wet."

"That doesn't make any sense," Christine pointed out. "How would a shark get so close?"

"It's supposed to be like, a megalodon, right?" Duncan asked.

"Yeah, don't worry about it," the director said. "Nobody cares how big the shark is. This is just a low-budget shark movie, nobody really pays attention. It's just pretend."

"Okay," Christine said.

"Okay, I guess," said Duncan.

"Okay, camera's rolling, you guys ready to film something?"

"Yeah!" they both cried. It was a lot better than walking through the woods.

"Okay, here's what you're gonna do, guys. In this scene, Duncan, you're gonna run up to Christine, okay, and you're gonna pick her up and you're gonna throw her in the water. But it's all gonna be in slow motion."

That one he really did come up with on the spot, and he was proud of himself for it, because it would be a creative way to pad that runtime.

"Basically, we do normal speed and then you put it in slow motion after?" Duncan asked.

The director was appalled that Duncan would think such a thing, and not sure what kind of fancy sets the actor had come out of. "No, no!" I don't know what kind of budget you think we have for this movie, but no. You're basically, you're going to run up to her and you're going to do all the actions, but you're going to act in slow motion."

"Cool," Duncan said. "Can I rip my shirt off?"

"Uh, maybe later. Alright, and action!"

Duncan growled as he lumber-acted toward Christine. Neither puppet was totally in frame. Christine turned and slowly bounced away.

"Alright everybody," the director called. "I said slow motion, okay? I don't know what that was, okay, but everybody back up. Back up. Even slower this time."

They backed up.

"Super slow," he directed. "Now, action!"

This time, he had a better shot of the lake behind his two actors. It was a pale blue that he thought would look nice and properly spooky with some roy-alty-free piano music added behind it in post.

Honestly, the slow motion shot sounded terrible, but it didn't look half bad.

Their speed picked up naturally once Christine had been tossed into the water, but the two of them seemed to be on a roll by that point, and the last thing any of them wanted to do was a dreaded third take.

She fell in the water and was stunned to see just how realistic the puppet shark looked. It didn't look at all like a silly, prop puppet shark. It looked like a real puppet shark, coming right at her real puppet body.

She swam away as dramatically as she could. The shark followed her, gnashing its many teeth.

It grabbed her arm and bit down. Hard.

She tried to scream, but water filled her mouth, and her felt tongue absorbed it. Only bubbles es-caped, with no sound.

"Eat dynamite you filthy shark!" Duncan screamed as he held up the dynamite, and lowered it again. He got distracted. He was looking over at Christine. "Gross, it's chewing on her."

He looked down at the prop dynamite he was supposed to throw, only to realize too late that it was real dynamite, and he was still holding it.

"Eep!"

It was the last single word response would ever give as he and the director were blown to smithereens.

Where Our "Heroes" Do Not Listen to Our Narrator, Me, Fisherman Fred

"Well, let it be a cautionary tale for you," I told the kids in conclusion. "There are plenty of scary things out there in the dark. Waiting. Watching."

I winked.

Most puppets can't wink, but I am probably one of the most advanced human puppets you've ever met.

"Anyway, have a fun night, kids."

Now, when I turned and left that tent, I was dang sure them kids were going to pack their things and head on home.

I wish they had.

I wish more than anything I could have spared them from the final terror of the night.

But I walked out of their tent, and they just kept right on with their night, like I had never even given them the hibby-jibbies.

"Man, he sure knows how to put the brakes on a fun evening," Chase said.

"I don't know," Grayson said in my defense. (Thank you, Grayson. That was sweet.)

As we have already established, he was the one of the two puppet brothers who was more inclined to like spookier stories.

"Well, I suppose so. It was a good story. And it had a shark in it."

What did I tell you? It works every time.

"Who doesn't like a shark story?"

Both boys nodded.

"You wanna hear another one?" Chance asked.

"Another shark story? Of course I do!"

Now that is the kind of enthusiasm a person ought to have for a story about sharks.

"This one starts with a mermaid."

"What?" Grayson demanded. "A *mermaid*? you said this was a shark story!"

"Yeah," Chance said in a huff, upset they had to go through this again. "Just let me get to that part."

Grayson was not convinced. "A… a mermaid, you say? Is this a *true* story?"

"Uh… of course it is."

Chance knew too well that the best stories were supposed to be true. Like the true story I'd just told them about the independent film crew. Chance must have known that would be a hard one to top, but it wasn't going to stop him from trying his best.

"Go for it," Grayson said.

"Okay. So a mermaid was singing her song…"

The Ballad of Mac the Shark
(as told by Chance, as told by me, Fisherman Fred)

Imagine, if you will, an old-timey club under the sea. Black and white, with a beautiful dame-puppet singing into her seashell mic. A spotlight blares on the wall behind her as her sweet voice rings out to the audience...

> *"My Bonnie lies over the ocean.*
> *My Bonnie lies over the sea.*
> *My Bonnie lies over the ocean.*
> *Oh, bring back my Bonnie to me.*
>
> *Bring back*
> *Bring back*
> *Bring back my Bonnie to me.*
>
> *To me!*
>
> *Bring back my Bonnie to me.*
> *Bring back*
> *Bring back*
>
> *Oh bring back my Bonnie to meeeeeeeee."*

Her name was Bubbles and she was a headliner at the Coral Club. She knew it was a dive, but she got to sing, and she loved working there. She used to love it. Until he took over.

Now.

Imagine a fierce looking puppet shark. He looks more or less like the puppet sharks you've seen already tonight in your mind, but you can tell he's different.

It's the little things.

The fishy grin as he shows off his top row of chompers. The cold malice in his dead, black eyes. The top hat.

"Hey there, doll face."

"Oh, hello, Mac."

"Nice pipes, doll face. Too bad the club is so empty."

That's Mac the shark, a two-bit card shark who won the club in a game of piranha poker. And then he ate the piranha.

"It doesn't help that you chow down on all the customers, Mac." Bubbles told him.

It was true that the Coral Club was becoming a real grim place to be. But Bubbles was telling Mac truths he didn't want to hear, and Mac was not the kind of shark who liked to hear things he didn't want to hear.

So, he did what any shark would do in his position, and he asked delicately for improvement.

"Yeah, about that. The grouper was pretty good, but the squid was tough. I'm not a squid guy, doll face. I'm more of a caviar guy. Can't you get some sturgeon in here?"

"I'm on my own here, Mac," Bubbles protested. "Sturgeon will come for a full band, but you ate all my musicians."

"A guy's gotta eat! Now, what I gotta eat depends on you, doll face. I never tried mermaid before, but I hear it's kinda like chicken of the sea."

"Mac! You wouldn't!"

But he would, and that was the cold hard truth of things.

"Try me."

Even Bubbles knew better than to do that. "A-alright, Mac. I'll do better. I promise. I'll bring in more customers. And I'll use my siren song to keep them mesmerized."

She would have said anything to keep that shark off her tail, and Mac took to the idea like a barnacle to a boat.

"Now that's more like it, doll face. You bring me the sushi, and you live to see another day."

"I understand."

"Good. But you need to find a new lighting guy."

She gasped. "No! You ate Ernie, too?"

"What can I say? I was in the mood for some light dessert. Get it?"

She got it alright.

"See you tomorrow, doll face. Right around dinner time."

So Bubbles talked to her sound man, Kurt. She found him working at a different, safer club, but felt she had no choice but to drag him down into the depths once more. "Come on, Kurt. You gotta help me! I've gotta look good on stage to lure customers in!"

"No can do, Bubbles. Look at what happened to Ernie. I don't want to up Mac's lunch."

"Neither do I! That's why I need your help. I'll pay you double what you get here."

"I don't know," Kurt said. It was good money, but was it worth his life?

"Triple?"

Well that certainly was.

"Well, I do have to pay for the kids' school, and that's a lotta clams."

"That's the spirit! Do it for the minnows?"

"Alright," he relented, "I'll do it. But if Mac starts smacking his lips or looks at me funny…"

"Thanks, Kurt! I'll see you tonight."

"You'll smell me first," he warned. "I'll be wearing lots of shark repellent. Lots and lots."

So Bubbles was well lit when she took the stage once more.

> *"Find me a man*
> *I'll say I love him*
> *Even if I don't.*
> *Find me a man*
> *I'll say I'll be there for him*
> *Even if I won't*
>
> *Find me a man*
> *Who'll cry for me*
> *Who'll be a standup guy for me*
> *Perhaps someone who'll lie*
> *For me*
> *Just find me a maaaaaan.*
>
> *Find me a man*
> *I'll call him handsome*
> *Even if he ain't*
> *Find me a man*
> *A walkin' checkbook*
> *With the patience of a saint*
>
> *Find me a man*

Who'll lie for me
Provide an alibi for me
Perhaps someone who'll die
For me

A doting angel who knows how to treat me
  right
A tender lover with a wanton appetite
Find me a fella who can keep me warm at
  night

Just...

Find me a...

Maaaaaaaaaaaaaaaaan."

Bubbles held the whole audience captive with her sweet words and sultry tone. The plentiful crowd swayed in harmony to her song, and Mac approached her as the final note rang out.

"Now, that's more like it, doll face! You'd better retire to your dressing room until your next set."

Bubbles swam off, but did not miss the screams of the various fishes whose lives she'd doomed. That sound would haunt her all her days.

She couldn't help but cry in front of her mirror. "What have I done? Mac is a monster." She knew she was a monster now as well. It didn't sound like anyone survived the carnage by the stage.

"But what else can I do?" she sobbed. "If I don't lure in more customers, Mac is gonna make a meal out of me."

But she couldn't keep feeding him forever as she had done that night, for Bubbles knew she could never survive the guilt for long. "I have to find a way out of this."

That was when Kurt came in to give her the curtain call. "You're on in fifteen minutes, Bubbles."

"Kurt!" she exclaimed. "You're alive!"

"Yeah," he said. "Mac filled up on customer fillets. I lived to light another day."

"I'm sorry I dragged you into this, Kurt."

"I knew what I was getting into. And together, we have a better chance at never becoming Mac's lunch."

"I'm going to find a way out of this, Kurt. I promise."

"I believe you, Bubbles. But until then, the show must go on!"

She nodded, knowing he was right.

And that's how it was. Night after night. Kurt would throw her in the spotlight, and she would bring in the new fish. Until one day, there was a knock on the door to her dressing room.

"Kurt?" she called.

"Nah," Mac said, entering without a proper invitation. He saw the whole club as his property, including her space. "It's me, doll face."

"Oh," Bubbles stammered — for one could never feel too at ease when a shark has just made himself at home in their dressing room. "H-hi, Mac. You usually don't see me before a show."

"Yeah, but tonight is special. I got something to discuss with you."

Bubbles knew that it was going to be more bad news. "What's the matter?" she asked. She knew she'd been netting plenty of fish with her voice, so she couldn't imagine there were any complaints there. "I've been bringing in good hauls."

"Yeah, yeah," Mac agreed. The chum's been great. But I've got a bigger vision for this place...

and a bigger appetite. Point is, I'm looking to expand."

Bubbles' heart sank. "Expand?"

"Yeah, we gotta bring in a whale. Every card shark joint worth its sea salt brings in a whale."

"A whale? Wow. That's a big ask, Mac."

Though they both knew full well he wasn't really asking.

"Are you saying you can't do it?"

"No, no. I can do it. Only, whales need more than a siren song to lure them in. I need to make a whale song."

"A whale what?"

"A whale song. When a mermaid sings a whale song, the whale can't resist. Only I don't have any lyrics. And I have to write some."

Mac had to think it over, but even to him the request sounded reasonable. Mac was prepared to muster a little bit of patience if it meant pulling in a whale. "Alright, doll face. You compose your little whale song and bring the big fish to me."

"Mammal," she corrected.

"What?" Mac snapped. Being patient had put him in a bad mood already.

"Mammal. A whale is a mammal."

"Fish, mammal, I don't care. It all goes in here," he laughed. "Get it? Ha ha, I kill me. Oh, and uh, Bubbles?"

"Yes, Mac?"

"You have two weeks. Or the menu will feature big Kurt, washed down with Bubbles. Comprende?"

Before she knew it, those two weeks were over.

"All ready for tonight, doll face?" Mac asked her before she took the stage.

"I'm ready," Bubbles told him, even though she felt awfully nervous about her plan.

"So this song is gonna fetch me a whale?"

Bubbles hoped it would do more than that.

"Yes."

"Good. 'Cause all I had today was some Mahi-Mahi and I worked up a whale of an appetite. Do you get it? I kill me, heh-heh."

Bubbles sighed and shook her head. He couldn't be more comically evil. The good guys never laughed at their own jokes.

"I'm going to start singing now. You should wait outside. When the whale comes, it'll be too big to come into the club."

"Gotcha, doll face. This is gonna be the best meal ever."

She tested the mic, singing her usual scales before diving into the song that was her last salvation.

> *"Wha-aaaaah*
> *Aha Hooooah*
> *Whhhaaaaoaaa*
> *Aaaaaoaaaaoah*
> *Aaaaoooaoaoah*
> *Oooooooaaaaahmh*
>
> *WaahaaaAaah*
> *Ahghaaaaaaah*
> *AOoOoahhhha*
> *Ahhhahhhhhhh!"*

Before she even had to reprise the first chorus, the whale was on its way.

> *"WaahaaaAaah*
> *Ahghaaaaaaah*
> *AOoOoahhhha*
> *Ahhhahhhhhhh!"*

"I don't believe it!" Kurt exclaimed. He was manning the lights and had been doubtful when he first heart the deep, bellowing sounds that Bubbles was making. But he could feel the whale making waves in its rush over to the Coral Club. "It's working! Keep singing, Bubbles!'

> *"WhaaAahOooah*
> *AhahhhaaAh*
> *OohahhooAhah*
> *OheehahhaOhh"*

"That's it," Mac said, going to meet the approaching mammal halfway. "My delicious whale of a meal. Come to Mac!"

> *"OoooohhhhHOoh*
> *WaaahoahhaOhH*
> *Haaaaaowooooahaaaa*
> *Ehooooaweoooohhh"*

The whale looked even larger than Mac could have imagined. Larger than he was positive he could eat.

"Holy mackerel!" he exclaimed as he tried to figure out how he could eat the entire thing without having to worry about leftovers.

He barely had time to wonder if the whole scheme had been a bad idea before the giant puppet whale had swallowed that little puppet shark whole.

It didn't even seem to notice, nor did it slow down on its way to that beautiful song, leaving only Mac's hat floating in the water.

Bubbles claimed the top hat when she took proper ownership of the Coral Club after that night, and all agreed it looked better on her than it ever had on Mac.

She hired the whale to be the bouncer, and figured that it must have been enough to keep Mac away, because she never saw that two-bit card shark again.

So that's the ballad of Mac the shark.

If Only Someone Could Have Predicted There Would be a Shark in These Here Woods

It was too late and dark for even the owl to hoot by the time Chance finished his last tale.

"What kind of story was that?" Grayson demanded.

"It was a shark story," Chance answered.

This was when I came upon them again. I was doing another circuit of Shearer Park, and had expected to find the tent empty, or gone altogether. I was certainly not expecting to find the boys engaging in further shark story critique.

"Kind of. That was weird."

"What can I say? I ate too many marshmallows. I'm loaded with sugar."

Staying in the dangerous woods after I had warned them? Not appreciating a shark story? Eating too many marshmallows?

These kids were *asking* for trouble, and I could simply stay silent no longer. "Hey, kids."

They turned to look at me, and it was Grayson who spoke up first. "Fisherman Fred! You scared us."

"Sorry about that. Did you think about the warning I gave you?"

They didn't look too sure, not even Chance as he answered. "I guess. A little bit."

That was pretty disheartening to hear, honestly. "I thought I would scare you into leaving. But it looks like you were determined to stay."

They said nothing.

Eventually I felt like I had to say *more*. "I warned you about the dangers of the woods."

They just stared at me. Like I was *crazy*. Like I was *paranoid*. Like I hadn't walked into the woods to give them a warning, risking my own secrets to try and keep those two little puppets safe.

"I told you about the vicious shark in the area. Now it seems you must learn the truth. The shark…"

I paused here for dramatic effect. That was a little trick you may have heard about earlier from Chance, but see now how the master employs this technique.

I've been waiting to use it this entire time!

While I was pausing for dramatic effect I was also gripping my head, preparing to speak "…is me!"

I straightened up and ripped off my puppet human head to reveal my puppet shark head.

Both boys gasped in horror.

"What?" they both asked in unison.

"That's right! I'm the shark that hunts these nearby waters. I am constantly hungry for the meat of human victims."

"Whaaat?" they asked, once again in unison.

And then.

Then.

Chance said something that really boiled my waters. "But that doesn't make any sense."

Can you believe?

The nerve!

Faced with a real life puppet shark, this kid is

telling me *to my face* that I don't make any *sense*. And then his brother decided to pile on!

"Why are you on land?"

They started taking turns!

"Why do you talk?"

"What's the need for the disguise?"

"Where do you get your clothes?"

I was outraged!

"No more questions," I told them.

"But that doesn't make any sense," Chance said again.

"Make *sense*?" I demanded. "Why does everything have to make sense?"

They didn't have an answer for that, and that was fine by me. I had *plenty* more to say. "People are obsessed with things needing to make sense. *Life* doesn't make sense. Nothing that has happened for the last seventy odd pages has made a lick of sense."

Still nothing.

So I continued.

"Who really cares? Can't we just have fun? Can't things just be weird for the sake of being weird? Anyway, have a drink. Make a friend. Stop worrying about things making sense."

"'Kay, geez," Chance said. He brushed it off like I had not just given him the most profound advice he'd ever heard from a puppet shark still-half encased in a puppet human disguise. "What a grouch."

I mean.

Ow.

That hurt.

I have *feelings*, you know. Not a lot of puppets realize this, but puppet sharks do have feelings. And I don't think they ever would have talked to me this dismissively when they thought I was a puppet human. They would never have called Fisherman Fred a grouch.

"So what happens now?" Grayson asked.

"Now?" I was still wounded, but after a moment his question snapped me back to reality. To the grim climax this night had been building to. "Oh, now. Now I'm gonna eat you."

Now, I know what you're thinking.

Isn't it rough to eat a couple kids just because they hurt my feelings?

Well, no. It isn't.

But I'll have you know that's not why I decided to eat them. I decided to do it because I'm a puppet shark, and they're puppet humans, and that's just how it all worked out.

But Chance looked as appalled as you probably look right now behind your page, reading about my plans from the comfort of your home. "What? Are you sure?"

"Yep." And you there, human judgy-pants with your book, I want you to take careful note of what I said next before you paint me as some sort of monster. "But to be sporting, I'll give you a thirty second head start."

"Thirty seconds?" Grayson demanded.

"Starting now," I clarified.

The brothers looked at each other. They thought for a moment. Then they screamed. They're running through the woods of Shearer Park as we speak.

I reckon I gave them even longer than thirty seconds by this point, so I guess I'd better stop narrating and start eating some puppets.

Oh, and as for you…

CHOMP!

FIN

The following pages feature images from the film as well as behind-the-scenes images. Used by permission.

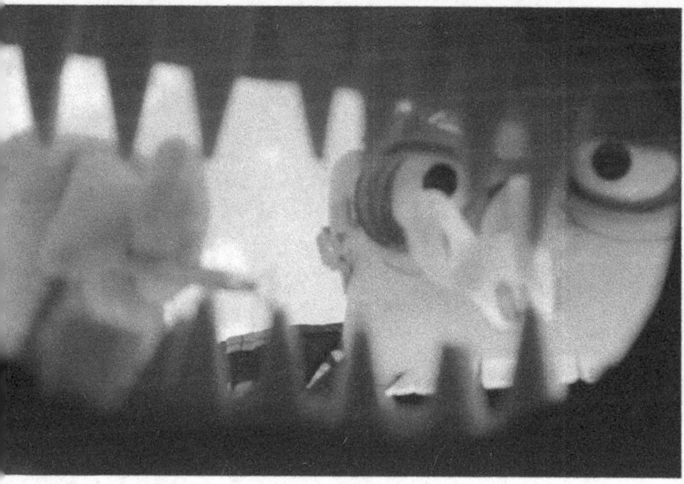

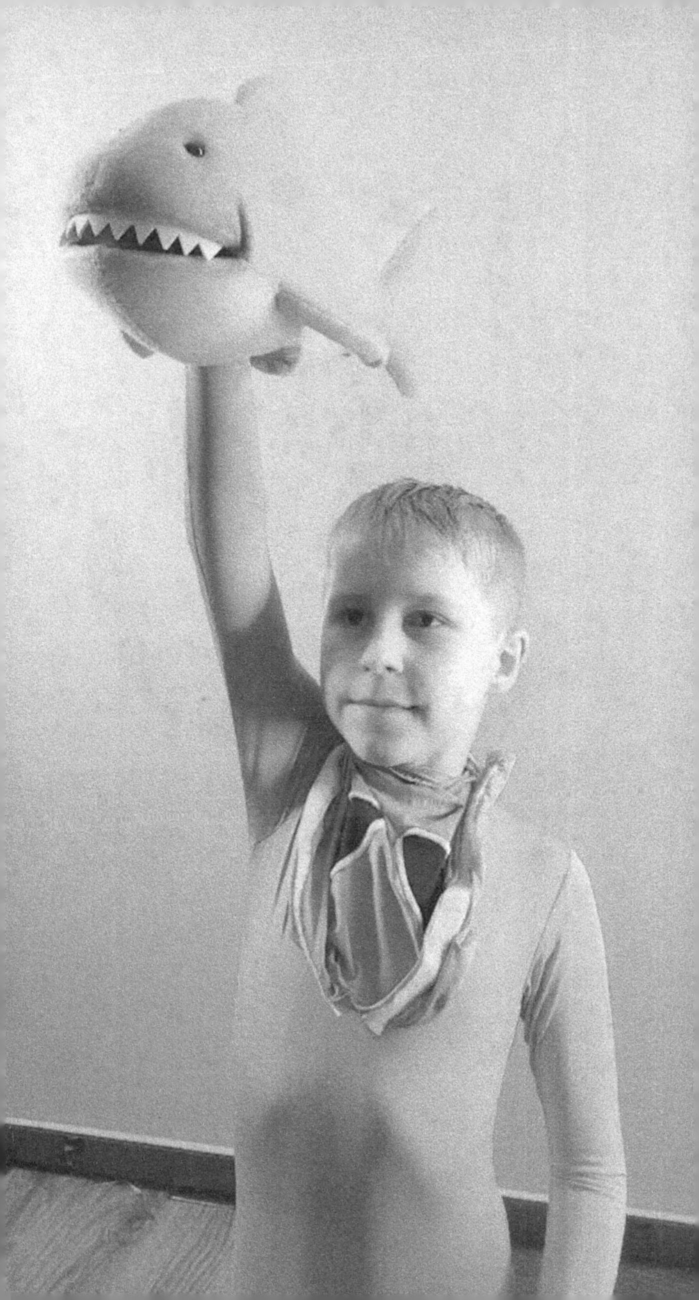

Epilogue

...

...

psst.

hey. hey you.

reader.

i've got something for you. a little post-acknowledgements scene if you will. a sort of epilogue.

don't worry.

i'm not fisherman fred.

you can trust me.

and you wanna know what happened to grayson and chance don't you?

don't you?

i'll tell you...

a stuffed puppet shark, complete with its fisherman hat hung on the white wall of the living room, observed by a very clever and lucky reader just before they take notice of two familiar puppets in the room.

"wow. it sure was lucky of us to beat fisherman fred," chance told his brother.

"yeah," grayson said. "i don't think i'm going camping anytime soon."

"hey, isn't this a weird book to have an epilogue?"

"uh, yeah."

"gee! it just occurred to me. didn't fisherman fred once say that he had an offspring?"

and then they both heard me knocking at the door.

"oh no!"

what do you think reader?

will all three of you be as lucky now as you were when you faced...

...

...

[pause for dramatic effect]

...

my father???!!!

Acknowledgments

(Please imagine that the song "If You Can't Do What's Right (Do What's Left)" by Gelatin Skelatin is playing as you read this page. If you don't know it, please visit www.gelatinskelatin.com for the full experience.)

There are so many people I want to thank for making this book happen. Brian G. Berry, who writes some of the best shark books I've ever read and who taught me how to pursue novelization projects. Ruth Anna Evans, my super talented cover designer. Tasha Reynolds, the best editor in the whole world.

Also Darren Stevens, Veronica D'Arc, Grayson Kelly, Chance Kelly, Teresa Pike, Brett Kelly, Anne-Marie Kelly, Adam Goldberg, Trever Payer, Chad Walls, Kim Fletcher, Amber Peters, Anne-Marie Frigon and Funsters.

Please   check   out www.facebook.com/funsterspuppets.

Additional writing credits go to Janet Hetherington and Trevor Payer who wrote the script, with additional dialogue from Miles Long. I preserved as much of the dialogue as was humanly possible (would that I could be so perfect as a puppet.)

Finally, a huge thanks to Ron Bonk who made this

movie possible, and trusted me with this book for some reason.

About the Author

Cat Voleur is a writer of dark fiction and host of two podcasts, Slasher Radio and The Nic F'n Woo Cage Cast. When she is not creating or consuming morbid content (or whatever you call this) you can most likely find her with her army of rescued felines, pursuing her passion for fictional languages.

She ask that you please remember only the featured image of her moving forward.

Also By Cat Voleur

Cat Voleur, despite being a very silly person generally, has never published any work like this before. If you enjoyed this book, we must implore you not to seek out the following titles, which are darker and scarier and far more serious. (Mostly.)

- Revenge Arc
- All of These People Are Going to Die 4: Heck House
- The Silence of the Lamps
- Kill Your Darlings